WILL SPRING BE EARLY?

or Will Spring Be Late?

WILL SPRING BE EARLY?

or Will Spring Be Late?

CROCKETT JOHNSON

HarperTrophy

A Division of HarperCollins*Publishers*

Will Spring Be Early?

or Will Spring Be Late?

WILL SPRING BE EARLY?

or Will Spring Be Late?

It was the second morning of February. The woods and the fields were covered with snow. The wind blew from a cold gray sky.

"This is the day!" said a voice from under the ground. "This is the day I make my prediction! . . . *Will spring be early or will spring be late?*"

8

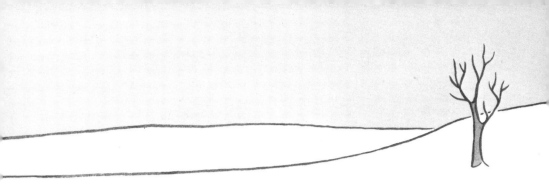

The voice came from a hole in
the middle of the field.

It was the Groundhog, coming
up out of his tunnel, talking to
himself.

"If I don't see my shadow spring will be *early*. I can go right out and spread the glad tidings."

The Groundhog's nose came

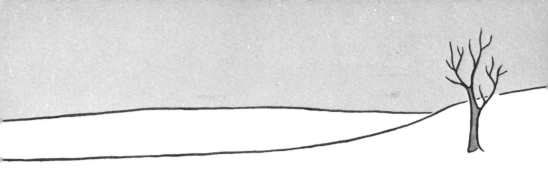

up in the hole, pausing there.

"But if I *do* see my shadow
I'll go back in my tunnel. It
will mean bad news. Spring
will be *late* this year."

The Groundhog shivered.
"How nice it is that I am
expected to stay out only when
I have *good* news," he said as
he raised himself up onto his

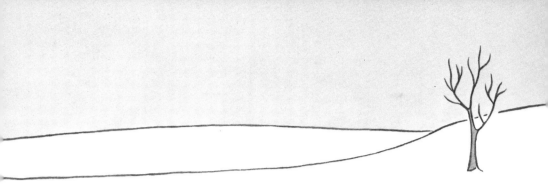

front paws. "Nobody wants to
hear of a late spring."

He looked at the gray sky.

"No shadows today!" he said.
"Spring will be *early!*"

He hopped out of the hole.
"I must tell the animals! It
will please them all, even the
grouchy Pig who sneers at my
predictions."

He started off, and stopped.
"Wait," he said. "Spring is
an important matter. I must be
certain there is no sun. I must
make *sure* I have no shadow."

He tried to smell the sun. He
raised his ears and listened for
it. But all he smelled or heard
was a truck on the road at the
edge of the field.

The road was beyond the end
of the Groundhog's world. He
paid no attention to the truck
or to the words on it that read
"Artificial Flower Co., Inc."

As the truck rounded a bend
in the road, a red flower flew
from it. The flower sailed high
across the field on the wintry
wind.

"No sun, and no shadow,"
the Groundhog was saying to
himself as he examined the
snow at his feet. "Definitely,
an early spring."

Smiling, he set off toward
the woods where most of the
animals slept during the cold
winter.

"How delighted they will

be when I tell them," he said.
"My prediction will spread joy
throughout the land."

And he hopped along happily,
humming a spring song.

Suddenly he halted.

There, with its stem in the snow, was a bright red flower, in full bloom.

The Groundhog stared at it.

His eyes grew wide and his
mouth opened.

"Spring," he whispered.

Then he shouted.

"Spring! It's here *now!"*

He broke into a run.

"I *never* have made a better prediction than this! Even the Pig will congratulate me."

He yelled through the woods.

"Spring is here!" he shouted.
"Spring?" said the Badger.
"The Groundhog said so!" the
Dormouse cried, dancing around
in the snow.

"Spring?" said the Skunk. "Is it really spring?"

"The Groundhog said so," said the Rabbit, hopping with joy and skidding on a patch of ice.

The Squirrel stuffed the last of
his acorns into his mouth. With
a carefree cheer he jumped from
his hollow tree and landed in a
snowdrift.

"Spring!" yelled the Chipmunk.
"Thanks to the Groundhog!"

"The Good Predictor!" cheered
the Raccoon, holding out a paw as
the Groundhog ran by.

"Spring is *here!*" the Groundhog
kept shouting, in a voice that was
becoming rather hoarse. "I predict
spring is here *now!*"

He ran on, to the Bear's cave.

When the Bear woke up and
heard what the Groundhog was
saying he roared in delight.

"Groundhog, you do better
every year! Spring! Spring in

February! Splendid! What
would we do without you?"

"I don't know," said the
Groundhog, swelling up his
chest as he ran off.

At last he came to the Pig.
The shouting and cheering had
waked the Pig and now he was
grumpily rooting under a tree
stump for breakfast.

"Spring! Spring! It is *here!*"
the Groundhog shouted loudly in
the Pig's ear.

"Harrummf?" said the Pig.

"Spring," said the Groundhog.

With his mouth full of frozen
roots the Pig turned around and
glared at the Groundhog.

"Look," he said, snorting and
thrusting his snout toward the

windswept field. "Snow! Ice!"

"It-it's sp-pr-ring," said the
Groundhog, suddenly shivering.

"Go away," said the Pig, and
he went back to his rooting.

The Groundhog went back to
the other animals.

"Spring really *is* here," he
said. "Come. Let me show you."

"Of course spring is here,"

said the Rabbit. "You *said* so."

"And you are always right,"
the Bear said. "If you were not,
we wouldn't believe in you."

"Come," said the Groundhog.

The animals followed him to
the field, where they saw the red
flower in full bloom.

It was more than they needed
to see. They danced in a circle

around it and shouted in praise
of spring and of the Groundhog.

The Pig stopped rooting for
breakfast and came over to see
what was going on.

The happy animals watched
him as he trotted up to the red
flower.

"You see?" the Groundhog
said. "Spring is here."

"Harrummf," said the Pig,
staring at the flower.

Then he rooted it up out of
the snow, took it in his mouth,
and chomped on it.

He tossed the flower aside.
"The leaves are paper. The
stem is wire. The petals are
plastic," he said. "And the lot
of you will freeze out here."

As he left he glanced at the
sky and at the Groundhog.

"I have a prediction to make,"
he said. "It's going to snow."

It began to snow.

Shivering, the animals looked
at the twisted flower. And they
looked at one another.

The Groundhog began to creep
quietly away.

"Just a moment!" bellowed the Bear. "There is some explaining to be done! Who is the *cause* of this? Why are we out here in a freezing snowstorm?"

"We were celebrating spring,"
said the Chipmunk.

"We were all so happy," the
Dormouse said, "until the Pig
came and chewed the flower."

"Precisely!" shouted the Bear. "And now we're cold and miserable and ridiculous! It's perfectly clear who's to blame!"

The animals nodded.

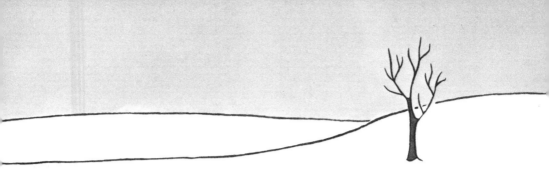

They blamed the Pig, of course.

And, on the second morning of
every February, the Groundhog
continues to make his prediction.

. . . *Will spring be early or will
spring be late?*